Tomie dePaola's
BOOK OF
BIBLE
STORIES

NEW INTERNATIONAL VERSION

G·P·Putnam's Sons/Zondervan
New York

For Karen and Harlow Carlson
who know the true meaning of friendship
— TdeP

Text copyright © 1990 by the Zondervan Corporation,
taken from the Holy Bible, New International Version.
Copyright © 1973, 1978, 1984 by International Bible Society.
Illustrations copyright © 1990 by Tomie dePaola.
All rights reserved. This book, or parts thereof, may not be
reproduced in any form without permission in writing from the publisher.
G. P. Putnam's Sons, a division of The Putnam & Grosset Group,
200 Madison Avenue, New York, NY 10016.
Published simultaneously in Canada.
Printed in Hong Kong by South China Printing Co. (1988) Ltd.

Library of Congress Cataloging-in-Publication Data   Bible. English. New
International. Selections 1988. Tomie dePaola's book of Bible stories.
Summary: A collection of Bible stories, from Creation to the Resurrection
of Christ and the appearance of the Holy Spirit at Pentecost. Includes index.
1. Bible stories, English. [1. Bible stories] I. DePaola, Tomie. II. Title.
III. Title: Book of Bible stories. BS391.2.D4   1988   220.9' 505   88-26468
ISBN 0-399-21690-1   (Putnam edition)
7   9   10   8
ISBN 0-310-91235-0   (Zondervan edition)
3   5   7   9   10   8   6   4   2

Book design by Nanette Stevenson. Calligraphy by Jeanyee Wong.

The wolf will live with the lamb,
   the leopard will lie down with the goat,
the calf and the lion and the yearling together;
   and a little child will lead them.

Isaiah 11:6

Contents

The wolf will live with the lamb / 5

The Old Testament / 9

God Creates the World / 11

Adam and Eve Disobey God / 15

Cain and Abel / 18

Noah and the Great Flood / 21

The Tower of Babel / 27

Abraham Offers Isaac to God / 28

Pharaoh's Daughter Finds Moses / 32

Moses and the Burning Bush / 35

The Israelites Cross the Red Sea / 39

Moses Receives the Ten Commandments / 43

The Fall of Jericho / 48

Samson and His Great Strength / 50

Naomi and Ruth / 57

David and Goliath / 59

Esther Saves Her People / 64

Daniel in the Den of Lions / 68

Jonah and the Great Fish / 73

The Lord Is My Shepherd / 76

The Lord Watches Over You / 78

Let Everything Praise the Lord / 79

The New Testament / 81

An Angel Visits Mary / 83

Jesus Is Born / 84

The Visit of the Magi / 88

The Boy Jesus at the Temple / 93

Jesus Is Baptized / 94

Jesus Feeds the Five Thousand / 96

Jesus Walks on the Water / 99

The Transfiguration / 100

The Story of the Good Samaritan / 102

Jesus Enters Jerusalem / 104

The Lord's Supper / 106

Jesus Prays at Gethsemane / 110

Jesus Dies on the Cross / 113

The Resurrection / 118

The Holy Spirit Comes at Pentecost / 120

Love Is Most Important / 122

Praise the Lord Everywhere / 124

Index of Bible Text / 126

THE OLD TESTAMENT

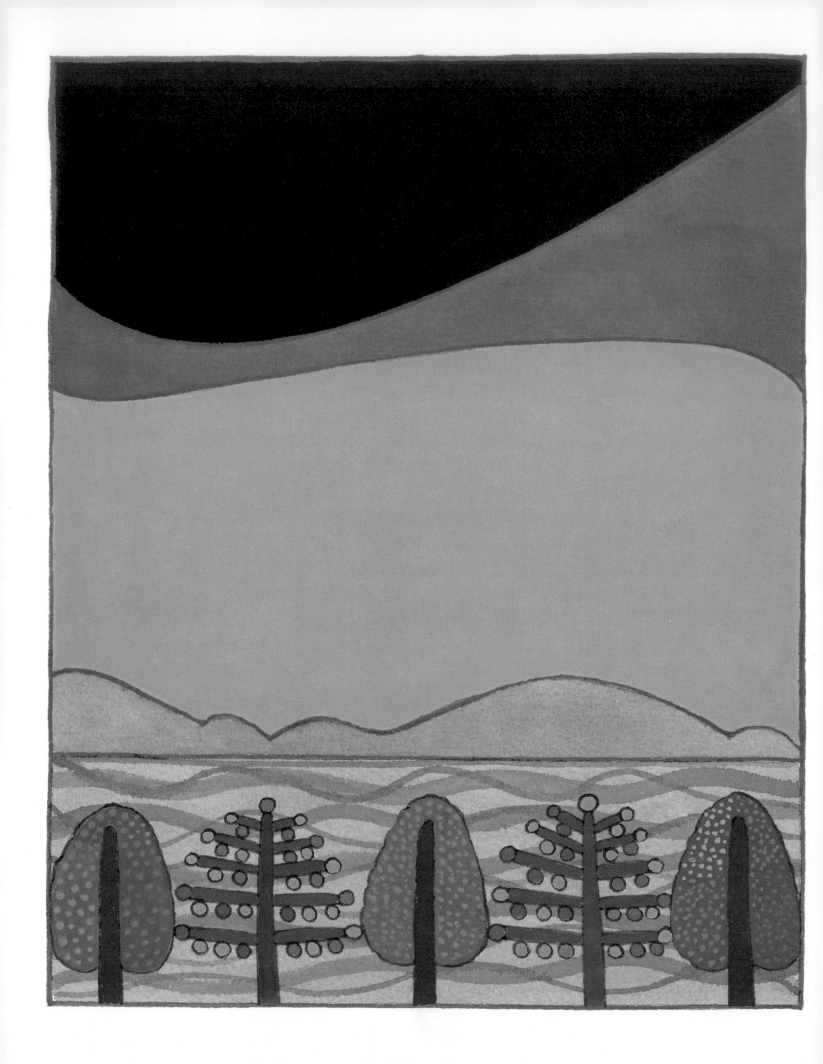

God Creates the World

In the beginning God created the heavens and the earth.

And God said, "Let there be light," and there was light. God saw that the light was good, and he separated the light from the darkness. God called the light "day," and the darkness he called "night." And there was evening, and there was morning—the first day.

And God said, "Let there be an expanse between the waters to separate water from water." God called the expanse "sky." And there was evening, and there was morning—the second day.

And God said, "Let the water under the sky be gathered to one place, and let dry ground appear." And it was so. God called the dry ground "land," and the gathered waters he called "seas." And God saw that it was good.

Then God said, "Let the land produce vegetation: seed-bearing plants and trees on the land that bear fruit with seed in it, according to their various kinds." And it was so. And there was evening, and there was morning—the third day.

And God said, "Let there be lights in the expanse of the sky to separate the day from the night, and let them serve as signs to mark seasons and days and years." God made two great lights—the greater light to govern the day and the lesser light to govern the night. He also made the stars. God set them in the expanse of the sky to give light on the earth. And there was evening, and there was morning—the fourth day.

And God said, "Let the water teem with living creatures, and let birds fly above the earth across the expanse of the sky." So God created the great creatures of the sea and every living and moving thing with which the water teems, according to their kinds, and every winged bird according to its kind. And God saw that it was good. And there was evening, and there was morning—the fifth day.

And God said, "Let the land produce living creatures according to their kinds: livestock, creatures that move along the ground, and wild animals, each according to its kind." And it was so.

Then God said, "Let us make man in our image, in our likeness, and let them rule over the fish of the sea and the birds of the air, over the livestock, over all the earth, and over all the creatures that move along the ground."

So God created man in his own image,
in the image of God he created him;
male and female he created them.

God blessed them and said to them, "Be fruitful and increase in number; fill the earth and subdue it. Rule over the fish of the sea and the birds of the air and over every living creature that moves on the ground."

God saw all that he had made, and it was very good. And there was evening, and there was morning—the sixth day.

Thus the heavens and the earth were completed in all their vast array.

By the seventh day God had finished the work he had been doing; so on the seventh day he rested from all his work. And God blessed the seventh day and made it holy, because on it he rested from all the work of creating that he had done.

Adam and Eve Disobey God

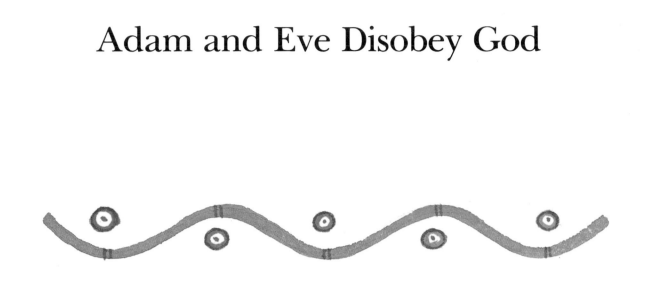

Now the serpent was more crafty than any of the wild animals the LORD God had made. He said to the woman, "Did God really say, 'You must not eat from any tree in the garden'?"

The woman said to the serpent, "We may eat fruit from the trees in the garden, but God did say, 'You must not eat fruit from the tree that is in the middle of the garden, and you must not touch it, or you will die.'"

"You will not surely die," the serpent said to the woman. "For God knows that when you eat of it your eyes will be opened, and you will be like God, knowing good and evil."

When the woman saw that the fruit of the tree was good for food and pleasing to the eye, and also desirable for gaining wisdom, she took some and ate it. She also gave some to her husband, who was with her, and he ate it. Then the eyes of both of them were opened, and they realized they were naked; so they sewed fig leaves together and made coverings for themselves.

Then the man and his wife heard the sound of the LORD God as he was walking in the garden in the cool of the day, and they hid from the LORD God among the trees of the garden. But the LORD God called to the man, "Where are you?"

He answered, "I heard you in the garden, and I was afraid because I was naked; so I hid."

And he said, "Who told you that you were naked? Have you eaten from the tree that I commanded you not to eat from?"

The man said, "The woman you put here with me—she gave me some fruit from the tree, and I ate it."

Then the LORD God said to the woman, "What is this you have done?"

The woman said, "The serpent deceived me, and I ate."

So the LORD God said to the serpent, "Because you have done this,

"Cursed are you above all the livestock
    and all the wild animals!
You will crawl on your belly
    and you will eat dust
    all the days of your life."

And the LORD God said, "The man has now become like one of us, knowing good and evil. He must not be allowed to reach out his hand and take also from the tree of life and eat, and live forever." So the LORD God banished him from the Garden of Eden to work the ground from which he had been taken.

Cain and Abel

Adam lay with his wife Eve, and she became pregnant and gave birth to Cain. She said, "With the help of the LORD I have brought forth a man." Later she gave birth to his brother Abel.

Now Abel kept flocks, and Cain worked the soil. In the course of time Cain brought some of the fruits of the soil as an offering to the LORD. But Abel brought fat portions from some of the firstborn of his flock. The LORD looked with favor on Abel and his offering, but on Cain and his offering he did not look with favor. So Cain was very angry, and his face was downcast.

Then the LORD said to Cain, "Why are you angry? Why is your face downcast?"

Now Cain said to his brother Abel, "Let's go out to the field." And while they were in the field, Cain attacked his brother Abel and killed him.

Then the LORD said to Cain, "Where is your brother Abel?"

"I don't know," he replied. "Am I my brother's keeper?"

The LORD said, "What have you done? Listen! Your brother's blood cries out to me from the ground. Now you are under a curse and driven from the ground, which opened its mouth to receive your brother's blood from your hand. When you work the ground, it will no longer yield its crops for you. You will be a restless wanderer on the earth."

Cain said to the LORD, "My punishment is more than I can bear. Today you are driving me from the land, and I will be hidden from your presence; I will be a restless wanderer on the earth, and whoever finds me will kill me."

But the LORD said to him, "Not so; if anyone kills Cain, he will suffer vengeance seven times over." Then the LORD put a mark on Cain so that no one who found him would kill him. So Cain went out from the LORD's presence and lived in the land of Nod, east of Eden.

Noah and the Great Flood

This is the account of Noah.

Noah was a righteous man, blameless among the people of his time, and he walked with God. Noah had three sons: Shem, Ham and Japheth.

So God said to Noah, "I am going to put an end to all people, for the earth is filled with violence because of them. I am surely going to destroy both them and the earth. So make yourself an ark of cypress wood; make rooms in it and coat it with pitch inside and out. I am going to bring floodwaters on the earth to destroy all life under the heavens, every creature that has the breath of life in it. Everything on earth will perish. But I will establish my covenant with you, and you will enter the ark—you and your sons and your wife and your sons' wives with you. You are to bring into the ark two of all living creatures, male and female, to keep them alive with you. You are to take every kind of food that is to be eaten and store it away as food for you and for them."

Noah did everything just as God commanded him.

And Noah and his sons and his wife and his sons' wives entered the ark to escape the waters of the flood. And after the seven days the floodwaters came on the earth. The waters rose and increased greatly on the earth, and the ark floated on the surface of the water. Every living thing on the face of the earth was wiped out; men and animals and the creatures that move along the ground and the birds of the air were wiped from the earth. Only Noah was left, and those with him in the ark.

The waters flooded the earth for a hundred and fifty days. But God remembered Noah and all the wild animals and the livestock that were with him in the ark, and he sent a wind over the earth, and the waters receded. The water receded steadily from the earth. At the end of the hundred and fifty days the water had gone down, and on the seventeenth day of the seventh month the ark came to rest on the mountains of Ararat.

After forty days Noah opened the window he had made in the ark and sent out a raven, and it kept flying back and forth until the water had dried up from the earth. Then he sent out a dove to see if the water had receded from the surface of the ground. But the dove could find no place to set its feet because there was water over all the surface of the earth; so it returned to Noah in the ark. He reached out his hand and took the dove and brought it back to himself in the ark. He waited seven more days and again sent out the dove from the ark. When the dove returned to him in the evening, there in its beak was a freshly plucked olive leaf! Then Noah knew that the water had receded from the earth. He waited seven more days and sent the dove out again, but this time it did not return to him.

By the first day of the first month of Noah's six hundred and first year, the water had dried up from the earth. Noah then removed the covering from the ark and saw that the surface of the ground was dry.

So Noah came out, together with his sons and his wife and his sons' wives. All the animals and all the creatures that move along the ground and all the birds—everything that moves on the earth—came out of the ark, one kind after another.

Then God said to Noah and to his sons with him: "I establish my covenant with you: Never again will all life be cut off by the waters of a flood; never again will there be a flood to destroy the earth. I have set my rainbow in the clouds, and it will be the sign of the covenant between me and the earth. Whenever I bring clouds over the earth and the rainbow appears in the clouds, I will remember my covenant between me and you and all living creatures of every kind. Never again will the waters become a flood to destroy all life."

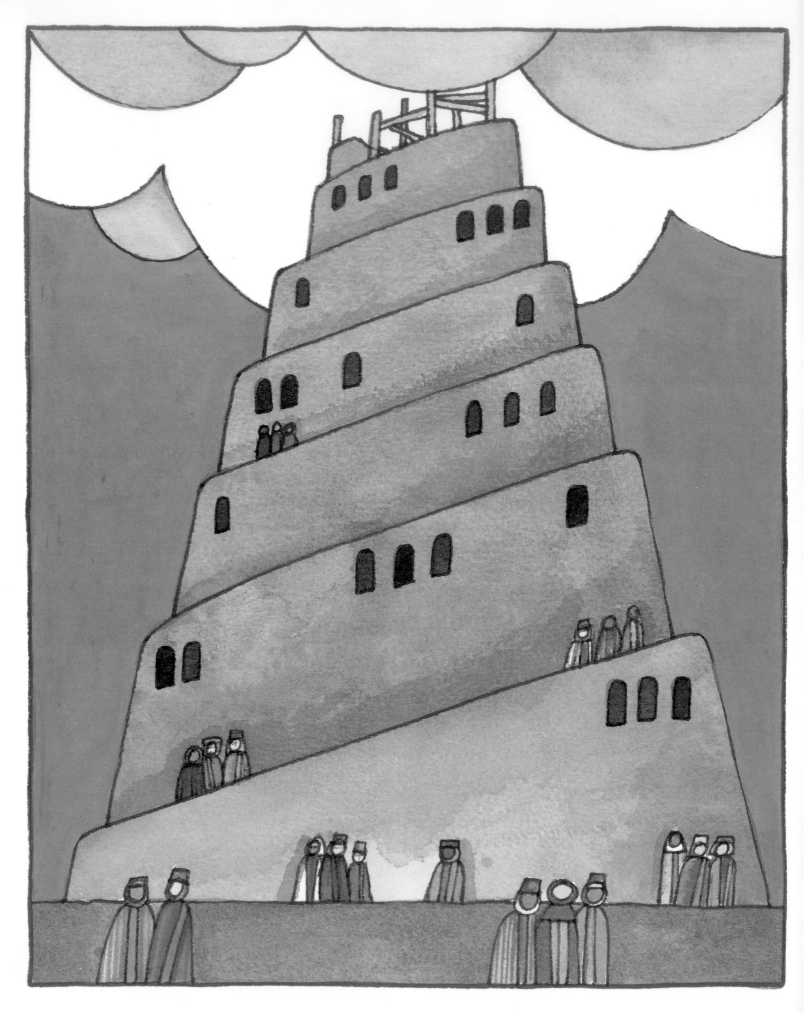

The Tower of Babel

God blessed Noah and his sons, saying to them, "Be fruitful and increase in number and fill the earth."

After the flood Noah lived 350 years. Altogether, Noah lived 950 years, and then he died.

Now the whole world had one language and a common speech. As men moved eastward, they found a plain in Shinar and settled there.

They said to each other, "Come, let's make bricks and bake them thoroughly." They used brick instead of stone, and tar for mortar. Then they said, "Come, let us build ourselves a city, with a tower that reaches to the heavens, so that we may make a name for ourselves and not be scattered over the face of the whole earth."

But the LORD came down to see the city and the tower that the men were building. The LORD said, "If as one people speaking the same language they have begun to do this, then nothing they plan to do will be impossible for them. Come, let us go down and confuse their language so they will not understand each other."

So the LORD scattered them from there over all the earth, and they stopped building the city. That is why it was called Babel—because there the LORD confused the language of the whole world. From there the LORD scattered them over the face of the whole earth.

Abraham Offers Isaac to God

God chose a man named Abraham and a woman named Sarah to be the parents of a special people who would be known as the Israelites. Even though Abraham and Sarah were very old, God promised them they would have a son, Isaac, who would carry on the family line.

Now the Lord was gracious to Sarah as he had said, and the Lord did for Sarah what he had promised. Sarah became pregnant and bore a son to Abraham in his old age, at the very time God had promised him. Abraham gave the name Isaac to the son Sarah bore him.

Some time later God tested Abraham. He said to him, "Abraham!"

"Here I am," he replied.

Then God said, "Take your son, your only son, Isaac, whom you love, and go to the region of Moriah. Sacrifice him there as a burnt offering on one of the mountains I will tell you about."

Early the next morning Abraham got up and saddled his donkey. He took with him two of his servants and his son Isaac. When he had cut enough wood for the burnt offering, he set out for the place God had told him about. On the third day Abraham looked up and saw the place in the distance. He said to his servants, "Stay here with the donkey while I and the boy go over there. We will worship and then we will come back to you."

Abraham took the wood for the burnt offering and placed it on his son Isaac, and he himself carried the fire and the knife. As the two of them went on together, Isaac spoke up and said to his father Abraham, "Father?"

"Yes, my son?" Abraham replied.

"The fire and wood are here," Isaac said, "but where is the lamb for the burnt offering?"

Abraham answered, "God himself will provide the lamb for the burnt offering, my son." And the two of them went on together.

When they reached the place God had told him about, Abraham built an altar there and arranged the wood on it. He bound his son Isaac and laid him on the altar, on top of the wood. Then he reached out his hand and took the knife to slay his son. But the angel of the LORD called out to him from heaven, "Abraham! Abraham!"

"Here I am," he replied.

"Do not lay a hand on the boy," he said. "Do not do anything to him. Now I know that you fear God, because you have not withheld from me your son, your only son."

Abraham looked up and there in a thicket he saw a ram caught by its horns. He went over and took the ram and sacrificed it as a burnt offering instead of his son. So Abraham called that place The LORD Will Provide. And to this day it is said, "On the mountain of the LORD it will be provided."

Pharaoh's Daughter Finds Moses

Many years passed. During a great famine Abraham's descendants moved to Egypt to find food. Eventually they became the slaves of Pharaoh but God still remembered his chosen people and was planning a way to set them free.

Now a man of the house of Levi married a Levite woman, and she became pregnant and gave birth to a son. When she saw that he was a fine child, she hid him for three months. But when she could hide him no longer, she got a papyrus basket for him and coated it with tar and pitch. Then she placed the child in it and put it among the reeds along the bank of the Nile. His sister stood at a distance to see what would happen to him.

Then Pharaoh's daughter went down to the Nile to bathe, and her attendants were walking along the river bank. She saw the basket among the reeds and sent her slave girl to get it. She opened it and saw the baby. He was crying, and she felt sorry for him. "This is one of the Hebrew babies," she said.

Then his sister asked Pharaoh's daughter, "Shall I go and get one of the Hebrew women to nurse the baby for you?"

"Yes, go," she answered. And the girl went and got the baby's mother. Pharaoh's daughter said to her, "Take this baby and nurse him for me, and I will pay you." So the woman took the baby and nursed him. When the child grew older, she took him to Pharaoh's daughter and he became her son. She named him Moses, saying, "I drew him out of the water."

Moses and the Burning Bush

Now Moses was tending the flock of Jethro his father-in-law, the priest of Midian, and he led the flock to the far side of the desert and came to Horeb, the mountain of God. There the angel of the LORD appeared to him in flames of fire from within a bush. Moses saw that though the bush was on fire it did not burn up. So Moses thought, "I will go over and see this strange sight—why the bush does not burn up."

When the LORD saw that he had gone over to look, God called to him from within the bush, "Moses! Moses!"

And Moses said, "Here I am."

"Do not come any closer," God said. "Take off your sandals, for the place where you are standing is holy ground." Then he said, "I am the God of your father, the God of Abraham, the God of Isaac and the God of Jacob." At this, Moses hid his face, because he was afraid to look at God.

The LORD said, "I have indeed seen the misery of my people in Egypt. I have heard them crying out because of their slave drivers, and I am concerned about their suffering. So I have come down to rescue them from the hand of the Egyptians and to bring them up out of that land into a good and spacious land, a land flowing with milk and honey. And now the cry of the Israelites has reached me, and I have seen the way the Egyptians are oppressing them. So now, go. I am sending you to Pharaoh to bring my people the Israelites out of Egypt."

But Moses said to God, "Who am I, that I should go to Pharaoh and bring the Israelites out of Egypt?"

And God said, "I will be with you. And this will be the sign to you that it is I who have sent you: When you have brought the people out of Egypt, you will worship God on this mountain."

Moses said to God, "Suppose I go to the Israelites and say to them, 'The God of your fathers has sent me to you,' and they ask me, 'What is his name?' Then what shall I tell them?"

God said to Moses, "I AM WHO I AM. This is what you are to say to the Israelites: 'I AM has sent me to you.'"

God also said to Moses, "Say to the Israelites, 'The LORD, the God of your fathers—the God of Abraham, the God of Isaac and the God of Jacob—has sent me to you.' This is my name forever, the name by which I am to be remembered from generation to generation. But I know that the king of Egypt will not let you go unless a mighty hand compels him. So I will stretch out my hand and strike the Egyptians with all the wonders that I will perform among them. After that, he will let you go."

Moses said to the LORD, "O Lord, I have never been eloquent, neither in the past nor since you have spoken to your servant. I am slow of speech and tongue."

The LORD said to him, "Who gave man his mouth? Who makes him deaf or mute? Who gives him sight or makes him blind? Is it not I, the LORD? Now go; I will help you speak and will teach you what to say."

But Moses said, "O Lord, please send someone else to do it."

Then the LORD's anger burned against Moses and he said, "What about your brother, Aaron the Levite? I know he can speak well. He is already on his way to meet you, and his heart will be glad when he sees you. You shall speak to him and put words in his mouth; I will help both of you speak and will teach you what to do. But take this staff in your hand so you can perform miraculous signs with it."

Then Moses went back to Jethro his father-in-law and said to him, "Let me go back to my own people in Egypt to see if any of them are still alive."

Jethro said, "Go, and I wish you well."

Now the LORD had said to Moses in Midian, "Go back to Egypt, for all the men who wanted to kill you are dead." So Moses took his wife and sons, put them on a donkey and started back to Egypt. And he took the staff of God in his hand.

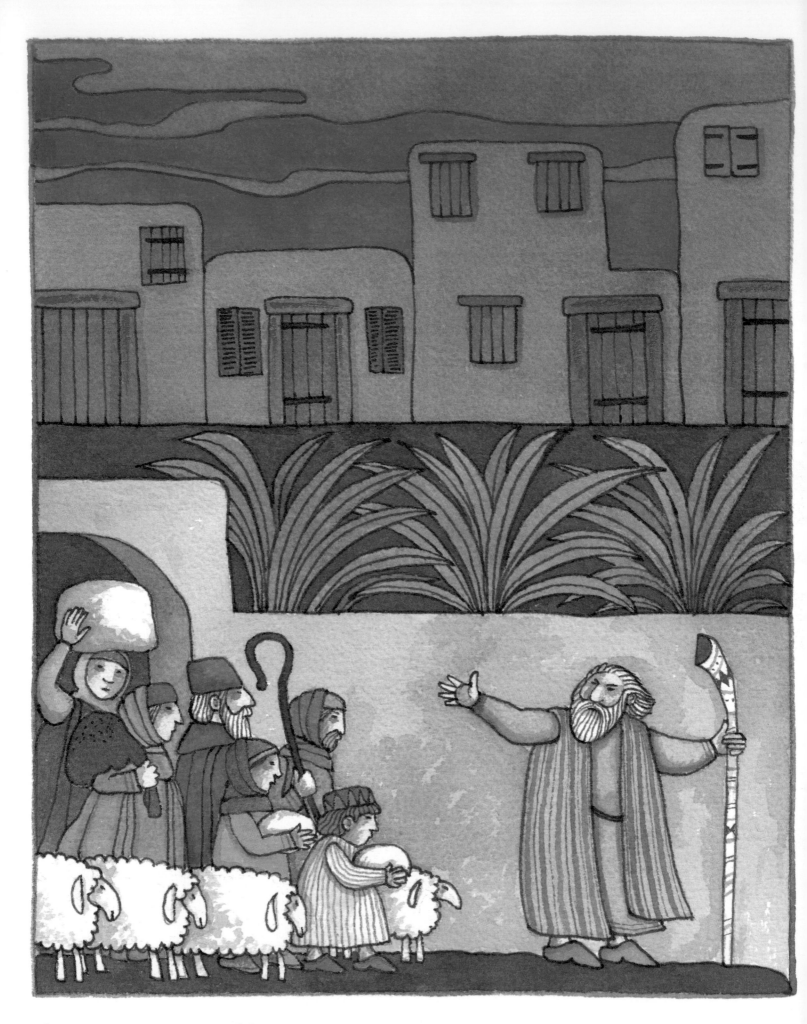

The Israelites Cross the Red Sea

Even after God sent nine horrible plagues, Pharaoh would not let the Hebrew people leave Egypt. But when God sent the tenth plague, which killed the firstborn male of every family, including Pharaoh's family, Pharaoh told Moses and the people to hurry and leave his country.

When the king of Egypt was told that the people had fled, Pharaoh and his officials changed their minds about them and said, "What have we done? We have let the Israelites go and have lost their services!" So he had his chariot made ready and took his army with him.

As Pharaoh approached, the Israelites looked up, and there were the Egyptians, marching after them. They were terrified and cried out to the LORD. They said to Moses, "Was it because there were no graves in Egypt that you brought us to the desert to die? What have you done to us by bringing us out of Egypt? Didn't we say to you in Egypt, 'Leave us alone; let us serve the Egyptians'? It would have been better for us to serve the Egyptians than to die in the desert!"

Moses answered the people, "Do not be afraid. Stand firm and you will see the deliverance the LORD will bring you today. The Egyptians you see today you will never see again. The LORD will fight for you; you need only to be still."

Then the angel of God, who had been traveling in front of Israel's army, withdrew and went behind them. The pillar of cloud also moved from in front and stood behind them, coming between the armies of Egypt and Israel. Throughout the night the cloud brought darkness to the one side and light to the other side; so neither went near the other all night long.

Then Moses stretched out his hand over the sea, and all that night the LORD drove the sea back with a strong east wind and turned it into dry land. The waters were divided, and the Israelites went through the sea on dry ground, with a wall of water on their right and on their left.

The Egyptians pursued them, and all Pharaoh's horses and chariots and horsemen followed them into the sea. During the last watch of the night the LORD looked down from the pillar of fire and cloud at the Egyptian army and threw it into confusion. He made the wheels of their chariots come off so that they had difficulty driving. And the Egyptians said, "Let's get away from the Israelites! The LORD is fighting for them against Egypt."

Then the LORD said to Moses, "Stretch out your hand over the sea so that the waters may flow back over the Egyptians and their chariots and horsemen." Moses stretched out his hand over the sea, and at daybreak the sea went back to its place. The Egyptians were fleeing toward it, and the LORD swept them into the sea. The water flowed back and covered the chariots and horsemen—the entire army of Pharaoh that had followed the Israelites into the sea. Not one of them survived.

That day the LORD saved Israel from the hands of the Egyptians, and Israel saw the Egyptians lying dead on the shore. And when the Israelites saw the great power the LORD displayed against the Egyptians, the people feared the LORD and put their trust in him and in Moses his servant.

Moses Receives the Ten Commandments

In the third month after the Israelites left Egypt—on the very day—they came to the Desert of Sinai. After they set out from Rephidim, they entered the Desert of Sinai, and Israel camped there in the desert in front of the mountain.

On the morning of the third day there was thunder and lightning, with a thick cloud over the mountain, and a very loud trumpet blast. Everyone in the camp trembled. Then Moses led the people out of the camp to meet with God, and they stood at the foot of the mountain. Mount Sinai was covered with smoke, because the LORD descended on it in fire. The smoke billowed up from it like smoke from a furnace, the whole mountain trembled violently, and the sound of the trumpet grew louder and louder. Then Moses spoke and the voice of God answered him.

And God spoke all these words:

"I am the LORD your God, who brought you out of Egypt, out of the land of slavery.

"You shall have no other gods before me.

"You shall not make for yourself an idol in the form of anything in heaven above or on the earth beneath or in the waters below.

"You shall not misuse the name of the LORD your God, for the LORD will not hold anyone guiltless who misuses his name.

"Remember the Sabbath day by keeping it holy.

"Honor your father and your mother, so that you may live long in the land the LORD your God is giving you.

"You shall not murder.

"You shall not commit adultery.

"You shall not steal.

"You shall not give false testimony against your neighbor.

"You shall not covet your neighbor's house. You shall not covet your neighbor's wife, or his manservant or maidservant, his ox or donkey, or anything that belongs to your neighbor."

When the people saw the thunder and lightning and heard the trumpet and saw the mountain in smoke, they trembled with fear.

The LORD said to Moses, "Come up to me on the mountain and stay here, and I will give you the tablets of stone, with the law and commands I have written for their instruction."

When Moses went up on the mountain, the cloud covered it, and the glory of the LORD settled on Mount Sinai. For six days the cloud covered the mountain, and on the seventh day the LORD called to Moses from within the cloud. Then Moses entered the cloud as he went on up the mountain. And he stayed on the mountain forty days and forty nights.

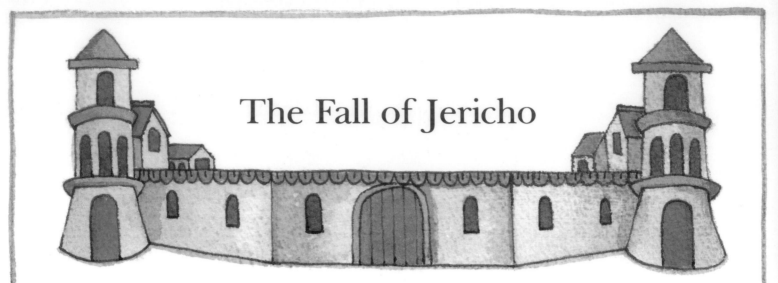

The Fall of Jericho

After forty years of wandering in the wilderness, the Israelites crossed the Jordan River into the land God had promised them. But before they could settle in their land they had to defeat their enemies and capture the cities.

Now Jericho was tightly shut up because of the Israelites. No one went out and no one came in.

Then the LORD said to Joshua, "See, I have delivered Jericho into your hands, along with its king and its fighting men. March around the city once with all the armed men. Do this for six days. Have seven priests carry trumpets of rams' horns in front of the ark. On the seventh day, march around the city seven times, with the priests blowing the trumpets."

So Joshua son of Nun called the priests and said to them, "Take up the ark of the covenant of the LORD and have seven priests carry trumpets in front of it." And he ordered the people, "Advance! March around the city, with the armed guard going ahead of the ark of the LORD." So he had the ark of the LORD carried around the city, circling it once. Then the people returned to camp and spent the night there. On the second day they marched around the city once and returned to the camp. They did this for six days.

On the seventh day, they got up at daybreak and marched around the city seven times in the same manner, except that on that day they circled the city seven times. The seventh time around, when the priests sounded the trumpet blast, Joshua commanded the people, "Shout! For the LORD has given you the city!"

When the trumpets sounded, the people shouted, and at the sound of the trumpet, when the people gave a loud shout, the wall collapsed; so every man charged straight in, and they took the city.

Then they burned the whole city and everything in it, but they put the silver and gold and the articles of bronze and iron into the treasury of the LORD's house. But Joshua spared Rahab the prostitute, with her family and all who belonged to her, because she hid the men Joshua had sent as spies to Jericho—and she lives among the Israelites to this day.

Samson and His Great Strength

Samson led Israel for twenty years in the days of the Philistines.

Some time later, he fell in love with a woman in the Valley of Sorek whose name was Delilah. The rulers of the Philistines went to her and said, "See if you can lure him into showing you the secret of his great strength and how we can overpower him so we may tie him up and subdue him. Each one of us will give you eleven hundred shekels [28 pounds] of silver."

So Delilah said to Samson, "Tell me the secret of your great strength and how you can be tied up and subdued."

Samson answered her, "If anyone ties me with seven fresh thongs that have not been dried, I'll become as weak as any other man."

Then the rulers of the Philistines brought her seven fresh thongs that had not been dried, and she tied him with them. With men hidden in the room, she called to him, "Samson, the Philistines are upon you!" But he snapped the thongs as easily as a piece of string snaps when it comes close to a flame. So the secret of his strength was not discovered.

Then Delilah said to Samson, "You have made a fool of me; you lied to me. Come now, tell me how you can be tied."

He said, "If anyone ties me securely with new ropes that have never been used, I'll become as weak as any other man."

So Delilah took new ropes and tied him with them. Then, with men hidden in the room, she called to him, "Samson, the Philistines are upon you!" But he snapped the ropes off his arms as if they were threads.

Delilah then said to Samson, "Until now, you have been making a fool of me and lying to me. Tell me how you can be tied."

He replied, "If you weave the seven braids of my head into the fabric on the loom and tighten it with the pin, I'll become as weak as any other man." So while he was sleeping, Delilah took the seven braids of his head, wove them into the fabric and tightened it with the pin.

Again she called to him, "Samson, the Philistines are upon you!" He awoke from his sleep and pulled up the pin and the loom, with the fabric.

Then she said to him, "How can you say, 'I love you,' when you won't confide in me? This is the third time you have made a fool of me and haven't told me the secret of your great strength." With such nagging she prodded him day after day until he was tired to death.

So he told her everything. "No razor has ever been used on my head," he said, "because I have been a Nazirite set apart to God since birth. If my head were shaved, my strength would leave me, and I would become as weak as any other man."

When Delilah saw that he had told her everything, she sent word to the rulers of the Philistines, "Come back once more; he has told me everything." So the rulers of the Philistines returned with the silver in their hands. Having put him to sleep on her lap, she called a man to shave off the seven braids of his hair, and so began to subdue him. And his strength left him.

Then she called, "Samson, the Philistines are upon you!"

He awoke from his sleep and thought, "I'll go out as before and shake myself free." But he did not know that the LORD had left him.

Then the Philistines seized him, gouged out his eyes and took him down to Gaza. Binding him with bronze shackles, they set him to grinding in the prison. But the hair on his head began to grow again after it had been shaved.

Now the rulers of the Philistines assembled to offer a great sacrifice to Dagon their god and to celebrate, saying, "Our god has delivered Samson, our enemy, into our hands."

While they were in high spirits, they shouted, "Bring out Samson to entertain us." So they called Samson out of the prison, and he performed for them.

When they stood him among the pillars, Samson said to the servant who held his hand, "Put me where I can feel the pillars that support the temple, so that I may lean against them." Now the temple was crowded with men and women; all the rulers of the Philistines were there, and on the roof were about three thousand men and women watching Samson perform. Then Samson prayed to the LORD, "O Sovereign LORD, remember me. O God, please strengthen me just once more, and let me with one blow get revenge on the Philistines for my two eyes." Then Samson reached toward the two central pillars on which the temple stood. Bracing himself against them, his right hand on the one and his left hand on the other, Samson said, "Let me die with the Philistines!" Then he pushed with all his might, and down came the temple on the rulers and all the people in it. Thus he killed many more when he died than while he lived.

Naomi and Ruth

In the days when the judges ruled, there was a famine in the land, and a man from Bethlehem in Judah, together with his wife and two sons, went to live for a while in the country of Moab. The man's name was Elimelech, his wife's name Naomi, and the names of his two sons were Mahlon and Kilion. They were Ephrathites from Bethlehem, Judah. And they went to Moab and lived there.

Now Elimelech, Naomi's husband, died, and she was left with her two sons. They married Moabite women, one named Orpah and the other Ruth. After they had lived there about ten years, both Mahlon and Kilion also died, and Naomi was left without her two sons and her husband.

When she heard in Moab that the LORD had come to the aid of his people by providing food for them, Naomi and her daughters-in-law prepared to return home from there. With her two daughters-in-law she left the place where she had been living and set out on the road that would take them back to the land of Judah.

Then Naomi said to her two daughters-in-law, "Go back, each of you, to your mother's home. May the LORD show kindness to you, as you have shown to your dead and to me. May the LORD grant that each of you will find rest in the home of another husband."

Then she kissed them and they wept aloud and said to her, "We will go back with you to your people."

But Naomi said, "Return home, my daughters. Why would you come with me? Am I going to have any more sons, who could become your husbands? Return home, my daughters; I am too old to have another husband. Even if I thought there was still hope for me—even if I had a husband tonight and then gave birth to sons—would you wait until they grew up? Would you remain unmarried for them? No, my daughters. It is more bitter for me than for you, because the LORD's hand has gone out against me!"

At this they wept again. Then Orpah kissed her mother-in-law good-by, but Ruth clung to her.

"Look," said Naomi, "your sister-in-law is going back to her people and her gods. Go back with her."

But Ruth replied, "Don't urge me to leave you or to turn back from you. Where you go I will go, and where you stay I will stay. Your people will be my people and your God my God. Where you die I will die, and there I will be buried. May the LORD deal with me, be it ever so severely, if anything but death separates you and me." When Naomi realized that Ruth was determined to go with her, she stopped urging her.

So Naomi returned from Moab accompanied by Ruth the Moabitess, her daughter-in-law, arriving in Bethlehem as the barley harvest was beginning.

Eventually Ruth married a man named Boaz. God blessed Ruth with a son, who became grandfather of the great King David.

David and Goliath

Now the Philistines gathered their forces for war and assembled at Socoh in Judah. Saul and the Israelites assembled and camped in the Valley of Elah and drew up their battle line to meet the Philistines. The Philistines occupied one hill and the Israelites another, with the valley between them.

A champion named Goliath, who was from Gath, came out of the Philistine camp. He was over nine feet tall. He had a bronze helmet on his head and wore a coat of scale armor of bronze weighing five thousand shekels [125 pounds]; on his legs he wore bronze greaves, and a bronze javelin was slung on his back. His spear shaft was like a weaver's rod, and its iron point weighed six hundred shekels [15 pounds]. His shield bearer went ahead of him.

Goliath stood and shouted to the ranks of Israel, "Why do you come out and line up for battle? Am I not a Philistine, and are you not the servants of Saul? Choose a man and have him come down to me. If he is able to fight and kill me, we will become your subjects; but if I overcome him and kill him, you will become our subjects and serve us." Then the Philistine said, "This day I defy the ranks of Israel! Give me a man and let us fight each other." On hearing the Philistine's words, Saul and all the Israelites were dismayed and terrified.

Now Jesse said to his son David, "Take this ephah [half a bushel] of roasted grain and these ten loaves of bread for your brothers and hurry to their camp. Take along these ten cheeses to the commander of their unit. See how your brothers are and bring back some assurance from them. They are with Saul and all the men of Israel in the Valley of Elah, fighting against the Philistines."

Early in the morning David left the flock with a shepherd, loaded up and set out, as Jesse had directed. He reached the camp as the army was going out to its battle positions, shouting the war cry. Israel and the Philistines were drawing up their lines facing each other. David left his things with the keeper of supplies, ran to the battle lines and greeted his brothers. As he was talking with them, Goliath, the Philistine champion from Gath, stepped out from his lines and shouted his usual defiance, and David heard it.

David said to Saul, "Let no one lose heart on account of this Philistine; your servant will go and fight him." Then he took his staff in his hand, chose five smooth stones from the stream, put them in the pouch of his shepherd's bag and, with his sling in his hand, approached the Philistine.

Meanwhile, the Philistine, with his shield bearer in front of him, kept coming closer to David. He looked David over and saw that he was only a boy, ruddy and handsome, and he despised him. He said to David, "Am I a dog, that you come at me with sticks?" And the Philistine cursed David by his gods. "Come here," he said, "and I'll give your flesh to the birds of the air and the beasts of the field!"

David said to the Philistine, "You come against me with sword and spear and javelin, but I come against you in the name of the LORD Almighty, the God of the armies of Israel, whom you have defied."

As the Philistine moved closer to attack him, David ran quickly toward the battle line to meet him. Reaching into his bag and taking out a stone, he slung it and struck the Philistine on the forehead. The stone sank into his forehead, and he fell facedown on the ground.

So David triumphed over the Philistine with a sling and a stone; without a sword in his hand he struck down the Philistine and killed him.

Esther Saves Her People

King Xerxes, ruler of Persia, chose Esther, a young Jewish woman, to be his queen. When Esther's cousin Mordecai heard that a man named Haman was trying to kill the Jewish people, he begged Esther to go to the king and ask for help.

On the third day Esther put on her royal robes and stood in the inner court of the palace, in front of the king's hall. The king was sitting on his royal throne in the hall, facing the entrance. When he saw Queen Esther standing in the court, he was pleased with her and held out to her the gold scepter that was in his hand. So Esther approached and touched the tip of the scepter.

Then the king asked, "What is it, Queen Esther? What is your request? Even up to half the kingdom, it will be given you."

Esther replied, "My petition and my request is this: If the king regards me with favor and if it pleases the king to grant my petition and fulfill my request, let the king and Haman come tomorrow to the banquet I will prepare for them. Then I will answer the king's question."

So the king and Haman went to dine with Queen Esther, and as they were drinking wine, the king again asked, "Queen Esther, what is your petition? It will be given you. What is your request? Even up to half the kingdom, it will be granted."

Then Queen Esther answered, "If I have found favor with you, O king, and if it pleases your majesty, grant me my life—this is my petition. And spare my people—this is my request. For I and my people have been sold for destruction and slaughter and annihilation. If we had merely been sold as male and female slaves, I would have kept quiet, because no such distress would justify disturbing the king."

King Xerxes asked Queen Esther, "Who is he? Where is the man who has dared to do such a thing?"

Esther said, "The adversary and enemy is this vile Haman."

Then Haman was terrified before the king and queen.

Harbona, one of the eunuchs attending the king, said, "A gallows seventy-five feet high stands by Haman's house. He had it made for Mordecai, who spoke up to help the king."

The king said, "Hang him on it!" So they hanged Haman on the gallows he had prepared for Mordecai. Then the king's fury subsided.

That same day King Xerxes gave Queen Esther the estate of Haman, the enemy of the Jews. And Mordecai came into the presence of the king, for Esther had told how he was related to her. The king took off his signet ring, which he had reclaimed from Haman, and presented it to Mordecai. And Esther appointed him over Haman's estate.

Esther again pleaded with the king, falling at his feet and weeping. She begged him to put an end to the evil plan of Haman the Agagite, which he had devised against the Jews. Then the king extended the gold scepter to Esther and she arose and stood before him.

King Xerxes replied to Queen Esther and to Mordecai the Jew, "Because Haman attacked the Jews, I have given his estate to Esther, and they have hanged him on the gallows. Now write another decree in the king's name in behalf of the Jews as seems best to you, and seal it with the king's signet ring—for no document written in the king's name and sealed with his ring can be revoked."

The king's edict granted the Jews in every city the right to assemble and protect themselves; to destroy, kill and annihilate any armed force of any nationality or province that might attack them and their women and children; and to plunder the property of their enemies. In every province and in every city, wherever the edict of the king went, there was joy and gladness among the Jews, with feasting and celebrating. And many people of other nationalities became Jews because fear of the Jews had seized them.

Daniel in the Den of Lions

It pleased Darius to appoint 120 satraps to rule throughout the kingdom, with three administrators over them, one of whom was Daniel. The satraps were made accountable to them so that the king might not suffer loss. Now Daniel so distinguished himself among the administrators and the satraps by his exceptional qualities that the king planned to set him over the whole kingdom. At this, the administrators and the satraps tried to find grounds for charges against Daniel in his conduct of government affairs, but they were unable to do so. They could find no corruption in him, because he was trustworthy and neither corrupt nor negligent. Finally these men said, "We will never find any basis for charges against this man Daniel unless it has something to do with the law of his God."

So the administrators and the satraps went as a group to the king and said: "O King Darius, live forever! The royal administrators, prefects, satraps, advisers and governors have all agreed that the king should issue an edict and enforce the decree that anyone who prays to any god or man during the next thirty days, except to you, O king, shall be thrown into the lions' den. Now, O king, issue the decree and put it in writing so that it cannot be altered—in accordance with the laws of the Medes and Persians, which cannot be repealed." So King Darius put the decree in writing.

Now when Daniel learned that the decree had been published, he went home to his upstairs room where the windows opened toward Jerusalem. Three times a day he got down on his knees and prayed, giving thanks to his God, just as he had done before. Then these men went as a group and found Daniel praying and asking God for help. So they went to the king and spoke to him about his royal decree: "Did you not publish a decree that during the next thirty days anyone who prays to any god or man except to you, O king, would be thrown into the lions' den?"

The king answered, "The decree stands—in accordance with the laws of the Medes and Persians, which cannot be repealed."

Then they said to the king, "Daniel, who is one of the exiles from Judah, pays no attention to you, O king, or to the decree you put in writing. He still prays three times a day." When the king heard this, he was greatly distressed; he was determined to rescue Daniel and made every effort until sundown to save him.

Then the men went as a group to the king and said to him, "Remember, O king, that according to the law of the Medes and Persians no decree or edict that the king issues can be changed."

So the king gave the order, and they brought Daniel and threw him into the lions' den. The king said to Daniel, "May your God, whom you serve continually, rescue you!"

A stone was brought and placed over the mouth of the den, and the king sealed it with his own signet ring and with the rings of his nobles, so that Daniel's situation might not be changed. Then the king returned to his palace and spent the night without eating and without any entertainment being brought to him. And he could not sleep.

At the first light of dawn, the king got up and hurried to the lions' den. When he came near the den, he called to Daniel in an anguished voice, "Daniel, servant of the living God, has your God, whom you serve continually, been able to rescue you from the lions?"

Daniel answered, "O king, live forever! My God sent his angel, and he shut the mouths of the lions. They have not hurt me, because I was found innocent in his sight. Nor have I ever done any wrong before you, O king."

The king was overjoyed and gave orders to lift Daniel out of the den. And when Daniel was lifted from the den, no wound was found on him, because he had trusted in his God.

Jonah and the Great Fish

The word of the LORD came to Jonah son of Amittai: "Go to the great city of Nineveh and preach against it, because its wickedness has come up before me."

But Jonah ran away from the LORD and headed for Tarshish. He went down to Joppa, where he found a ship bound for that port. After paying the fare, he went aboard and sailed for Tarshish to flee from the LORD.

Then the LORD sent a great wind on the sea, and such a violent storm arose that the ship threatened to break up. All the sailors were afraid and each cried out to his own god. And they threw the cargo into the sea to lighten the ship.

But Jonah had gone below deck, where he lay down and fell into a deep sleep. The captain went to him and said, "How can you sleep? Get up and call on your god! Maybe he will take notice of us, and we will not perish."

Then the sailors said to each other, "Come, let us cast lots to find out who is responsible for this calamity." They cast lots and the lot fell on Jonah.

So they asked him, "Tell us, who is responsible for making all this trouble for us? What do you do? Where do you come from? What is your country? From what people are you?"

He answered, "I am a Hebrew and I worship the LORD, the God of heaven, who made the sea and the land."

This terrified them and they asked, "What have you done?" (They knew he was running away from the LORD, because he had already told them so.)

The sea was getting rougher and rougher. So they asked him, "What should we do to you to make the sea calm down for us?"

"Pick me up and throw me into the sea," he replied, "and it will become calm. I know that it is my fault that this great storm has come upon you."

Instead, the men did their best to row back to land. But they could not, for the sea grew even wilder than before. Then they cried to the LORD, "O LORD, please do not let us die for taking this man's life. Do not hold us accountable for killing an innocent man, for you, O LORD, have done as you pleased." Then they took Jonah and threw him overboard, and the raging sea grew calm. At this the men greatly feared the LORD, and they offered a sacrifice to the LORD and made vows to him.

But the LORD provided a great fish to swallow Jonah, and Jonah was inside the fish three days and three nights.

From inside the fish, Jonah prayed to the LORD his God.

And the LORD commanded the fish and it vomited Jonah onto dry land.

Then the word of the LORD came to Jonah a second time: "Go to the great city of Nineveh and proclaim to it the message I give you."

Jonah obeyed the word of the LORD and went to Nineveh.

The Lord Is My
Shepherd

The LORD is my shepherd, I shall not be in want.
    He makes me lie down in green pastures,
he leads me beside quiet waters,
    he restores my soul.
He guides me in paths of righteousness
    for his name's sake.
Even though I walk
    through the valley of the shadow of death,
I will fear no evil,
    for you are with me;
your rod and your staff,
    they comfort me.

You prepare a table before me
    in the presence of my enemies.
You anoint my head with oil;
    my cup overflows.
Surely goodness and love will follow me
    all the days of my life,
and I will dwell in the house of the LORD
    forever.

The Lord Watches Over You

I lift up my eyes to the hills—
    where does my help come from?
My help comes from the LORD,
    the Maker of heaven and earth.

He will not let your foot slip—
    he who watches over you will not slumber;
indeed, he who watches over Israel
    will neither slumber nor sleep.

The LORD watches over you—
    the LORD is your shade at your right hand;
the sun will not harm you by day,
    nor the moon by night.

The LORD will keep you from all harm—
    he will watch over your life;
the LORD will watch over your coming and going
    both now and forevermore.

Let Everything Praise the Lord

Praise the LORD.

Praise God in his sanctuary;
  praise him in his mighty heavens.
Praise him for his acts of power;
  praise him for his surpassing greatness.
Praise him with the sounding of the trumpet,
  praise him with the harp and lyre,
praise him with tambourine and dancing,
  praise him with the strings and flute,
praise him with the clash of cymbals,
  praise him with resounding cymbals.

Let everything that has breath praise the LORD.

Praise the LORD.

THE NEW TESTAMENT

An Angel Visits Mary

In the sixth month, God sent the angel Gabriel to Nazareth, a town in Galilee, to a virgin pledged to be married to a man named Joseph, a descendant of David. The virgin's name was Mary. The angel went to her and said, "Greetings, you who are highly favored! The Lord is with you."

Mary was greatly troubled at his words and wondered what kind of greeting this might be. But the angel said to her, "Do not be afraid, Mary, you have found favor with God. You will be with child and give birth to a son, and you are to give him the name Jesus. He will be great and will be called the Son of the Most High. The Lord God will give him the throne of his father David, and he will reign over the house of Jacob forever; his kingdom will never end."

"How will this be," Mary asked the angel, "since I am a virgin?"

The angel answered, "The Holy Spirit will come upon you, and the power of the Most High will overshadow you. So the holy one to be born will be called the Son of God. Even Elizabeth your relative is going to have a child in her old age, and she who was said to be barren is in her sixth month. For nothing is impossible with God."

"I am the Lord's servant," Mary answered. "May it be to me as you have said." Then the angel left her.

Jesus Is Born

In those days Caesar Augustus issued a decree that a census should be taken of the entire Roman world. (This was the first census that took place while Quirinius was governor of Syria.) And everyone went to his own town to register.

So Joseph also went up from the town of Nazareth in Galilee to Judea, to Bethlehem the town of David, because he belonged to the house and line of David. He went there to register with Mary, who was pledged to be married to him and was expecting a child. While they were there, the time came for the baby to be born, and she gave birth to her firstborn, a son. She wrapped him in cloths and placed him in a manger, because there was no room for them in the inn.

And there were shepherds living out in the fields nearby, keeping watch over their flocks at night. An angel of the Lord appeared to them, and the glory of the Lord shone around them, and they were terrified. But the angel said to them, "Do not be afraid. I bring you good news of great joy that will be for all the people. Today in the town of David a Savior has been born to you; he is Christ the Lord. This will be a sign to you: You will find a baby wrapped in cloths and lying in a manger."

Suddenly a great company of the heavenly host appeared with the angel, praising God and saying,

"Glory to God in the highest,
and on earth peace to men on whom his favor rests."

When the angels had left them and gone into heaven, the shepherds said to one another, "Let's go to Bethlehem and see this thing that has happened, which the Lord has told us about."

So they hurried off and found Mary and Joseph, and the baby, who was lying in the manger. When they had seen him, they spread the word concerning what had been told them about this child, and all who heard it were amazed at what the shepherds said to them. But Mary treasured up all these things and pondered them in her heart. The shepherds returned, glorifying and praising God for all the things they had heard and seen, which were just as they had been told.

The Visit of the Magi

After Jesus was born in Bethlehem in Judea, during the time of King Herod, Magi from the east came to Jerusalem and asked, "Where is the one who has been born king of the Jews? We saw his star in the east and have come to worship him."

When King Herod heard this he was disturbed, and all Jerusalem with him. When he had called together all the people's chief priests and teachers of the law, he asked them where the Christ was to be born. "In Bethlehem in Judea," they replied, "for this is what the prophet has written:

"'But you, Bethlehem, in the land of Judah,
    are by no means least among the rulers of Judah;
for out of you will come a ruler
    who will be the shepherd of my people Israel.'"

Then Herod called the Magi secretly and found out from them the exact time the star had appeared. He sent them to Bethlehem and said, "Go and make a careful search for the child. As soon as you find him, report to me, so that I too may go and worship him."

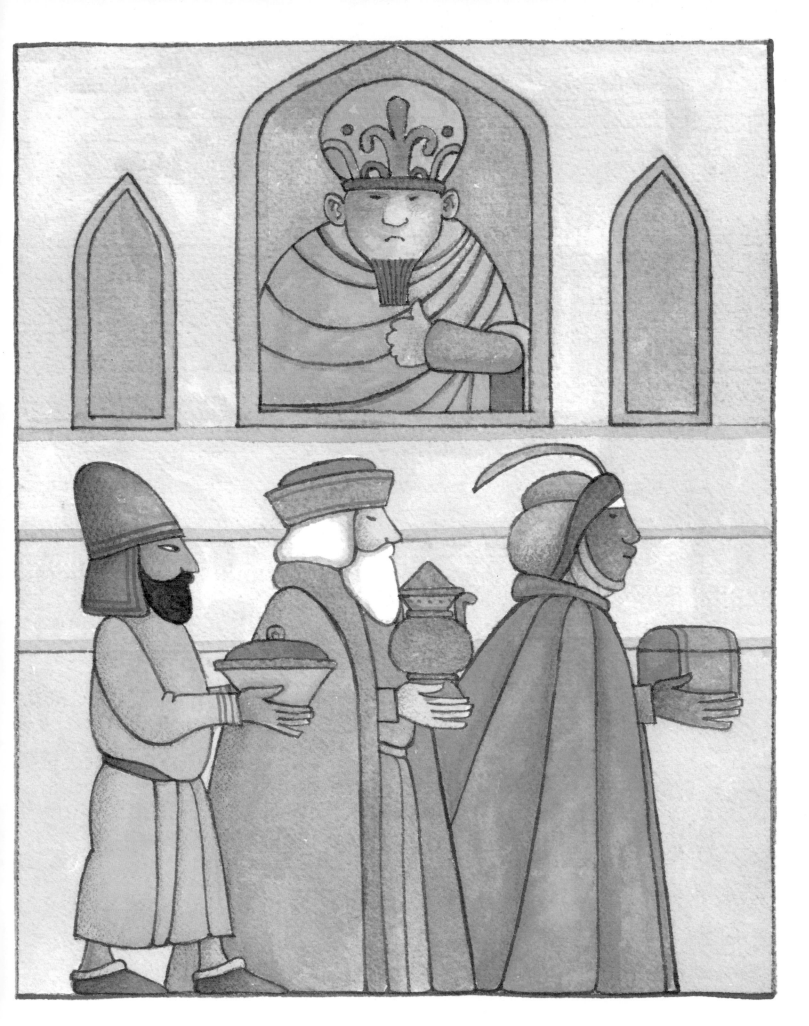

After they had heard the king, they went on their way, and the star they had seen in the east went ahead of them until it stopped over the place where the child was. When they saw the star, they were overjoyed. On coming to the house, they saw the child with his mother, Mary, and they bowed down and worshiped him. Then they opened their treasures and presented him with gifts of gold and of incense and of myrrh. And having been warned in a dream not to go back to Herod, they returned to their country by another route.

The Boy Jesus at the Temple

Every year Jesus' parents went to Jerusalem for the Feast of the Passover. When he was twelve years old, they went up to the Feast, according to the custom. After the Feast was over, while his parents were returning home, the boy Jesus stayed behind in Jerusalem, but they were unaware of it. Thinking he was in their company, they traveled on for a day. Then they began looking for him among their relatives and friends. When they did not find him, they went back to Jerusalem to look for him. After three days they found him in the temple courts, sitting among the teachers, listening to them and asking them questions. Everyone who heard him was amazed at his understanding and his answers. When his parents saw him, they were astonished. His mother said to him, "Son, why have you treated us like this? Your father and I have been anxiously searching for you."

"Why were you searching for me?" he asked. "Didn't you know I had to be in my Father's house?" But they did not understand what he was saying to them.

Then he went down to Nazareth with them and was obedient to them. But his mother treasured all these things in her heart. And Jesus grew in wisdom and stature, and in favor with God and men.

Jesus Is Baptized

During the high priesthood of Annas and Caiaphas, the word of God came to John son of Zechariah in the desert. He went into all the country around the Jordan, preaching a baptism of repentance for the forgiveness of sins. As is written in the book of the words of Isaiah the prophet:

"A voice of one calling in the desert,
'Prepare the way for the Lord,
    make straight paths for him.
Every valley shall be filled in,
    every mountain and hill made low.
The crooked roads shall become straight,
    the rough ways smooth.
And all mankind will see God's salvation.'"

The people were waiting expectantly and were all wondering in their hearts if John might possibly be the Christ. John answered them all, "I baptize you with water. But one more powerful than I will come, the thongs of whose sandals I am not worthy to untie. He will baptize you with the Holy Spirit and with fire. His winnowing fork is in his hand to clear his threshing floor and to gather the wheat into his barn, but he will burn up the chaff with unquenchable fire." And with many other words John exhorted the people and preached the good news to them.

When all the people were being baptized, Jesus was baptized too. And as he was praying, heaven was opened and the Holy Spirit descended on him in bodily form like a dove. And a voice came from heaven: "You are my Son, whom I love; with you I am well pleased."

Now Jesus himself was about thirty years old when he began his ministry.

Jesus Feeds the Five Thousand

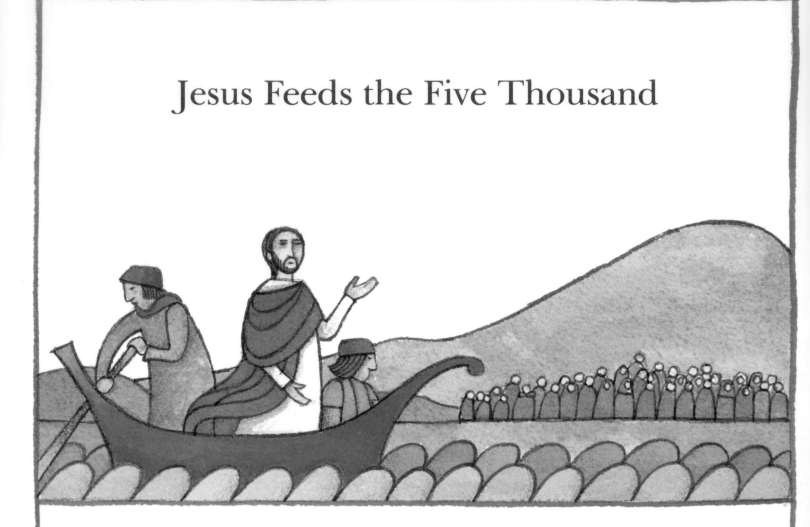

Some time after this, Jesus crossed to the far shore of the Sea of Galilee (that is, the Sea of Tiberias), and a great crowd of people followed him because they saw the miraculous signs he had performed on the sick. Then Jesus went up on a mountainside and sat down with his disciples. The Jewish Passover Feast was near.

When Jesus looked up and saw a great crowd coming toward him, he said to Philip, "Where shall we buy bread for these people to eat?" He asked this only to test him, for he already had in mind what he was going to do.

Philip answered him, "Eight months' wages would not buy enough bread for each one to have a bite!"

Another of his disciples, Andrew, Simon Peter's brother, spoke up, "Here is a boy with five small barley loaves and two small fish, but how far will they go among so many?"

Jesus said, "Have the people sit down." There was plenty of grass in that place, and the men sat down, about five thousand of them. Jesus then took the loaves, gave thanks, and distributed to those who were seated as much as they wanted. He did the same with the fish.

When they had all had enough to eat, he said to his disciples, "Gather the pieces that are left over. Let nothing be wasted." So they gathered them and filled twelve baskets with the pieces of the five barley loaves left over by those who had eaten.

Jesus Walks on the Water

Jesus made the disciples get into the boat and go on ahead of him to the other side, while he dismissed the crowd. After he had dismissed them, he went up on a mountainside by himself to pray. When evening came, he was there alone, but the boat was already a considerable distance from land, buffeted by the waves because the wind was against it.

During the fourth watch of the night Jesus went out to them, walking on the lake. When the disciples saw him walking on the lake, they were terrified. "It's a ghost," they said, and cried out in fear.

But Jesus immediately said to them: "Take courage! It is I. Don't be afraid."

"Lord, if it's you," Peter replied, "tell me to come to you on the water."

"Come," he said.

Then Peter got down out of the boat, walked on the water and came toward Jesus. But when he saw the wind, he was afraid and, beginning to sink, cried out, "Lord, save me!"

Immediately Jesus reached out his hand and caught him. "You of little faith," he said, "why did you doubt?"

And when they climbed into the boat, the wind died down. Then those who were in the boat worshiped him, saying, "Truly you are the Son of God."

The Transfiguration

After six days Jesus took with him Peter, James, and John, the brother of James, and led them up a high mountain by themselves. There he was transfigured before them. His face shone like the sun, and his clothes became as white as the light. Just then there appeared before them Moses and Elijah, talking with Jesus.

Peter said to Jesus, "Lord, it is good for us to be here. If you wish, I will put up three shelters—one for you, one for Moses and one for Elijah."

While he was still speaking, a bright cloud enveloped them, and a voice from the cloud said, "This is my Son, whom I love; with him I am well pleased. Listen to him!"

When the disciples heard this, they fell facedown to the ground, terrified. But Jesus came and touched them. "Get up," he said. "Don't be afraid." When they looked up, they saw no one except Jesus.

As they were coming down the mountain, Jesus instructed them, "Don't tell anyone what you have seen, until the Son of Man has been raised from the dead."

The disciples asked him, "Why then do the teachers of the law say that Elijah must come first?"

Jesus replied, "To be sure, Elijah comes and will restore all things. But I tell you, Elijah has already come, and they did not recognize him, but have done to him everything they wished. In the same way the Son of Man is going to suffer at their hands." Then the disciples understood that he was talking to them about John the Baptist.

The Story of
the Good Samaritan

On one occasion an expert in the law stood up to test Jesus. "Teacher," he asked, "what must I do to inherit eternal life?"

"What is written in the Law?" he replied. "How do you read it?"

He answered: "'Love the Lord your God with all your heart and with all your soul and with all your strength and with all your mind'; and, 'Love your neighbor as yourself.'"

"You have answered correctly," Jesus replied. "Do this and you will live."

But he wanted to justify himself, so he asked Jesus, "And who is my neighbor?"

In reply Jesus said: "A man was going down from Jerusalem to Jericho, when he fell into the hands of robbers. They stripped him of his clothes, beat him and went away, leaving him half dead. A priest happened to be going down the same road, and when he saw the man, he passed by on the other side. So too, a Levite, when he came to the place and saw him, passed by on the other side. But a Samaritan, as he traveled, came where the man was, and when he saw him, he took pity on him. He went to him and bandaged his wounds, pouring on oil and wine. Then he put the man on his own donkey, took him to an inn and took care of him. The next day he took out two silver coins and gave them to the innkeeper. 'Look after him,' he said, 'and when I return, I will reimburse you for any extra expense you may have.'

"Which of these three do you think was a neighbor to the man who fell into the hands of robbers?"

The expert in the law replied, "The one who had mercy on him."

Jesus told him, "Go and do likewise."

Jesus Enters Jerusalem

Jesus took the Twelve aside and told them what was going to happen to him. "We are going up to Jerusalem," he said, "and the Son of Man will be betrayed to the chief priests and teachers of the law. They will condemn him to death and will hand him over to the Gentiles, who will mock him and spit on him, flog him and kill him. Three days later he will rise."

As they approached Jerusalem and came to Bethphage and Bethany at the Mount of Olives, Jesus sent two of his disciples, saying to them, "Go to the village ahead of you, and just as you enter it, you will find a colt tied there, which no one has ever ridden. Untie it and bring it here. If anyone asks you, 'Why are you doing this?' tell him, 'The Lord needs it and will send it back here shortly.'"

They went and found a colt outside in the street, tied at a doorway. As they untied it, some people standing there asked, "What are you doing, untying that colt?" They answered as Jesus had told them to, and the people let them go. When they brought the colt to Jesus and threw their cloaks over it, he sat on it. Many people spread their cloaks on the road, while others spread branches they had cut in the fields. Those who went ahead and those who followed shouted,

"Hosanna!"

"Blessed is he who comes in the name of the Lord!"

"Blessed is the coming kingdom of our father David!"

"Hosanna in the highest!"

The Lord's Supper

On the first day of the Feast of Unleavened Bread, when it was customary to sacrifice the Passover lamb, Jesus' disciples asked him, "Where do you want us to go and make preparations for you to eat the Passover?"

So he sent two of his disciples, telling them, "Go into the city, and a man carrying a jar of water will meet you. Follow him. Say to the owner of the house he enters, 'The Teacher asks: Where is my guest room, where I may eat the Passover with my disciples?' He will show you a large upper room, furnished and ready. Make preparations for us there."

The disciples left, went into the city and found things just as Jesus had told them. So they prepared the Passover.

When evening came, Jesus arrived with the Twelve. While they were reclining at the table eating, he said, "I tell you the truth, one of you will betray me—one who is eating with me."

They were saddened, and one by one they said to him, "Surely not I?"

"It is one of the Twelve," he replied, "one who dips bread into the bowl with me. The Son of Man will go just as it is written about him. But woe to that man who betrays the Son of Man! It would be better for him if he had not been born."

While they were eating, Jesus took bread, gave thanks and broke it, and gave it to his disciples, saying, "Take it; this is my body."

Then he took the cup, gave thanks and offered it to them, and they all drank from it.

"This is my blood of the covenant, which is poured out for many," he said to them. "I tell you the truth, I will not drink again of the fruit of the vine until that day when I drink it anew in the kingdom of God."

Jesus Prays at Gethsemane

Jesus went with his disciples to a place called Gethsemane, and he said to them, "Sit here while I go over there and pray." He took Peter and the two sons of Zebedee along with him, and he began to be sorrowful and troubled. Then he said to them, "My soul is overwhelmed with sorrow to the point of death. Stay here and keep watch with me."

Going a little farther, he fell with his face to the ground and prayed, "My Father, if it is possible, may this cup be taken from me. Yet not as I will, but as you will."

Then he returned to his disciples and found them sleeping. "Could you men not keep watch with me for one hour?" he asked Peter. "Watch and pray so that you will not fall into temptation. The spirit is willing, but the body is weak."

He went away a second time and prayed, "My Father, if it is not possible for this cup to be taken away unless I drink it, may your will be done."

When he came back, he again found them sleeping, because their eyes were heavy. So he left them and went away once more and prayed the third time, saying the same thing.

Then he returned to the disciples and said to them, "Are you still sleeping and resting? Look, the hour is near, and the Son of Man is betrayed into the hands of sinners. Rise, let us go! Here comes my betrayer!"

While he was still speaking, Judas, one of the Twelve, arrived. With him was a large crowd armed with swords and clubs, sent from the chief priests and the elders of the people. Now the betrayer had arranged a signal with them: "The one I kiss is the man; arrest him." Going at once to Jesus, Judas said, "Greetings, Rabbi!" and kissed him.

Jesus replied, "Friend, do what you came for."

Then the men stepped forward, seized Jesus and arrested him.

Jesus Dies on the Cross

The governor's soldiers took Jesus into the Praetorium and gathered the whole company of soldiers around him. They stripped him and put a scarlet robe on him, and then twisted together a crown of thorns and set it on his head. They put a staff in his right hand and knelt in front of him and mocked him. "Hail, king of the Jews!" they said. They spit on him, and took the staff and struck him on the head again and again. After they had mocked him, they took off the robe and put his own clothes on him. Then they led him away to crucify him.

As they were going out, they met a man from Cyrene, named Simon, and they forced him to carry the cross. They came to a place called Golgotha (which means The Place of the Skull). There they offered Jesus wine to drink, mixed with gall, but after tasting it, he refused to drink it. When they had crucified him, they divided up his clothes by casting lots. And sitting down, they kept watch over him there. Above his head they placed the written charge against him: THIS IS JESUS, THE KING OF THE JEWS. Two robbers were crucified with him, one on his right and one on his left. Those who passed by hurled insults at him, shaking their heads and saying, "You who are going to destroy the temple and build it in three days, save yourself! Come down from the cross, if you are the Son of God!"

In the same way the chief priests, the teachers of the law and the elders mocked him. "He saved others," they said, "but he can't save himself! He's the King of Israel! Let him come down now from the cross, and we will believe in him. He trusts in God. Let God rescue him now if he wants him, for he said, 'I am the Son of God.'" In the same way the robbers who were crucified with him also heaped insults on him.

From the sixth hour until the ninth hour darkness came over all the land. About the ninth hour Jesus cried out in a loud voice, *"Eloi, Eloi, lama sabachthani?"*—which means, "My God, my God, why have you forsaken me?"

When some of those standing there heard this, they said, "He's calling Elijah."

Immediately one of them ran and got a sponge. He filled it with wine vinegar, put it on a stick, and offered it to Jesus to drink. The rest said, "Now leave him alone. Let's see if Elijah comes to save him."

And when Jesus had cried out again in a loud voice, he gave up his spirit.

At that moment the curtain of the temple was torn in two from top to bottom. The earth shook and the rocks split. The tombs broke open and the bodies of many holy people who had died were raised to life. They came out of the tombs, and after Jesus' resurrection they went into the holy city and appeared to many people.

When the centurion and those with him who were guarding Jesus saw the earthquake and all that had happened, they were terrified, and exclaimed, "Surely he was the Son of God!"

The Resurrection

After the Sabbath, at dawn on the first day of the week, Mary Magdalene and the other Mary went to look at the tomb.

There was a violent earthquake, for an angel of the Lord came down from heaven and, going to the tomb, rolled back the stone and sat on it. His appearance was like lightning, and his clothes were white as snow. The guards were so afraid of him that they shook and became like dead men.

The angel said to the women, "Do not be afraid, for I know that you are looking for Jesus, who was crucified. He is not here; he has risen, just as he said. Come and see the place where he lay. Then go quickly and tell his disciples: 'He has risen from the dead and is going ahead of you into Galilee. There you will see him.' Now I have told you."

So the women hurried away from the tomb, afraid yet filled with joy, and ran to tell his disciples. Suddenly Jesus met them. "Greetings," he said. They came to him, clasped his feet and worshiped him. Then Jesus said to them, "Do not be afraid. Go and tell my brothers to go to Galilee; there they will see me."

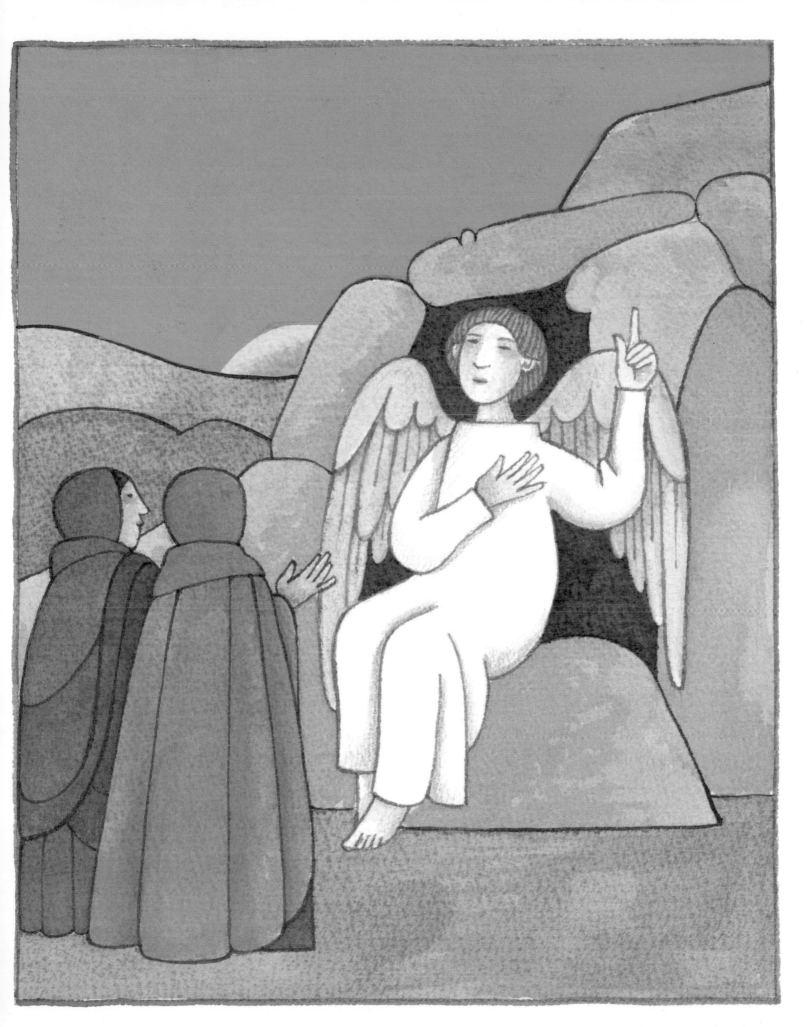

The Holy Spirit
Comes at Pentecost

When the day of Pentecost came, the disciples and those with them were all together in one place. Suddenly a sound like the blowing of a violent wind came from heaven and filled the whole house where they were sitting. They saw what seemed to be tongues of fire that separated and came to rest on each of them. All of them were filled with the Holy Spirit and began to speak in other tongues as the Spirit enabled them.

Now there were staying in Jerusalem God-fearing Jews from every nation under heaven. When they heard this sound, a crowd came together in bewilderment, because each one heard them speaking in his own language. Utterly amazed, they asked: "Are not all these men who are speaking Galileans? Then how is it that each of us hears them in his own native language?" Amazed and perplexed, they asked one another, "What does this mean?"

Some, however, made fun of them and said, "They have had too much wine."

Then Peter stood up with the Eleven, raised his voice and addressed the crowd: "Fellow Jews and all of you who live in Jerusalem, let me explain this to you; listen carefully to what I say. These men are not drunk, as you suppose. It's only nine in the morning! Therefore let all Israel be assured of this: God has made this Jesus, whom you crucified, both Lord and Christ."

When the people heard this, they were cut to the heart and said to Peter and the other apostles, "Brothers, what shall we do?"

Peter replied, "Repent and be baptized, every one of you, in the name of Jesus Christ for the forgiveness of your sins. And you will receive the gift of the Holy Spirit. The promise is for you and your children and for all who are far off—for all whom the Lord our God will call."

With many other words he warned them, and he pleaded with them, "Save yourselves from this corrupt generation." Those who accepted his message were baptized, and about three thousand were added to their number that day.

They devoted themselves to the apostles' teaching and to the fellowship, to the breaking of bread and to prayer.

Love Is Most Important

If I speak in the tongues of men and of angels, but have not love, I am only a resounding gong or a clanging cymbal. If I have the gift of prophecy and can fathom all mysteries and all knowledge, and if I have a faith that can move mountains, but have not love, I am nothing. If I give all I possess to the poor and surrender my body to the flames, but have not love, I gain nothing.

Love is patient, love is kind. It does not envy, it does not boast, it is not proud. It is not rude, it is not self-seeking, it is not easily angered, it keeps no record of wrongs. Love does not delight in evil but rejoices with the truth. It always protects, always trusts, always hopes, always perseveres.

Love never fails. But where there are prophecies, they will cease; where there are tongues, they will be stilled; where there is knowledge, it will pass away. For we know in part and we prophesy in part, but when perfection comes, the imperfect disappears. When I was a child, I talked like a child, I thought like a child, I reasoned like a child. When I became a man, I put childish ways behind me. Now we see but a poor reflection as in a mirror; then we shall see face to face. Now I know in part; then I shall know fully, even as I am fully known.

And now these three remain: faith, hope and love. But the greatest of these is love.

Praise the Lord Everywhere

Praise the LORD.
Praise the LORD from the heavens,
 praise him in the heights above.
Praise him, all his angels,
 praise him, all his heavenly hosts.
Praise him, sun and moon,
 praise him, all you shining stars.
Praise him, you highest heavens
 and you waters above the skies.
Let them praise the name of the LORD,
 for he commanded and they were created.
He set them in place for ever and ever;
 he gave a decree that will never pass away.

Praise the LORD from the earth,
 you great sea creatures and all ocean depths,
lightning and hail, snow and clouds,
 stormy winds that do his bidding,
you mountains and all hills,
 fruit trees and all cedars,
wild animals and all cattle,
 small creatures and flying birds,
kings of the earth and all nations,
 you princes and all rulers on earth,
young men and maidens,
 old men and children.

Let them praise the name of the LORD,
    for his name alone is exalted;
    his splendor is above the earth and the heavens.
He has raised up for his people a horn,
    the praise of all his saints,
    of Israel, the people close to his heart.

Praise the LORD.

Index of Bible Text

THE OLD TESTAMENT

God Creates the World
   Genesis 1:1, 3–6, 8–11, 13–14, 16–17,
   19–21, 23–24, 26–28, 31; 2:1–3
Adam and Eve Disobey God
   Genesis 3:1–14, 22–23
Cain and Abel
   Genesis 4:1–6, 8–16
Noah and the Great Flood
   Genesis 6:9–10, 13–14, 17–19, 21–22; 7:7,
   10, 18, 23–24; 8:1, 3–4, 6–13, 18–19; 9:8,
   11, 13–15
The Tower of Babel
   Genesis 9:1, 28–29; 11:1–9
Abraham Offers Isaac to God
   Genesis 21:1–3; 22:1–14
Pharaoh's Daughter Finds Moses
   Exodus 2:1–10
Moses and the Burning Bush
   Exodus 3:1–15, 19–20; 4:10–15, 17–20
The Israelites Cross the Red Sea
   Exodus 14:5–6, 10–14, 19–28, 30–31
Moses Receives the Ten Commandments
   Exodus 19:1–2, 16–19; 20:1–4, 7–8, 12–18;
   24:12, 15–16, 18
The Fall of Jericho
   Joshua 6:1–4, 6–7, 11, 14–16, 20, 24–25
Samson and His Great Strength
   Judges 15:20; 16:4–23, 25–30
Naomi and Ruth
   Ruth 1:1–18, 22
David and Goliath
   1 Samuel 17:1–11, 17–23, 32, 40–45,
   48–50
Esther Saves Her People
   Esther 5:1–3, 7–8; 7:1–6, 9–10
Daniel in the Den of Lions
   Daniel 6:1–23
Jonah and the Great Fish
   Jonah 1:1–17; 2:1, 10; 3:1–3a

The Lord Is My Shepherd
  Psalm 23:1–6
The Lord Watches Over You
  Psalm 121:1–8
Let Everything Praise the Lord
  Psalm 150:1–6

THE NEW TESTAMENT

An Angel Visits Mary
  Luke 1:26–38
Jesus Is Born
  Luke 2:1–20
The Visit of the Magi
  Matthew 2:1–12
The Boy Jesus at the Temple
  Luke 2:41–52
Jesus Is Baptized
  Luke 3:2–6, 15–18, 21–23
Jesus Feeds the Five Thousand
  John 6:1–13
Jesus Walks on the Water
  Matthew 14:22–33
The Transfiguration
  Matthew 17:1–8
The Story of the Good Samaritan
  Luke 10:25–37
Jesus Enters Jerusalem
  Mark 10:32–34; 11:1–10
The Lord's Supper
  Mark 14:12–26
Jesus Prays at Gethsemane
  Matthew 26:36–56
Jesus Dies on the Cross
  Matthew 27:27–54
The Resurrection
  Matthew 28:1–10
The Holy Spirit Comes at Pentecost
  Acts 2:1–8, 12–15, 36–42
Love Is Most Important
  1 Corinthians 13:1–13
Praise the Lord Everywhere
  Psalm 148:1–14